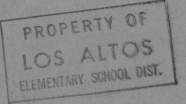

Tom and the Small Ant

by *Leonore Klein*
illustrated by *Harriet Sherman*

Alfred A. Knopf *New York*

To my mother with love / LK

For Frieda Chertkoff / HS

L.C. Catalog card number: 65-21568

THIS IS A BORZOI BOOK, PUBLISHED BY ALFRED A. KNOPF, INC.

Tom and the Small Ant

"Here I am," said Ant. "Away from home. All on my own for the very first time. I have walked all day. I have come a long way.

"What a great steep wall," said Ant. "I must be careful not to fall."

"Here I am," said Tom. "Here I am in the same old spot. And it's just as hot as it was yesterday. What is there to do?" asked Tom. "Nothing new!"

"What a fine tall tree," said Ant. "Could there be something sweet on top for me? Should I try to climb it? How it sways in the wind!

"Swing, swing, sway, sway. Oh, this is such a worrisome day," said Ant.

"Here is that same old rose," said Tom. "I'll smell that same old rose with my same old nose. Same old smell," said Tom.

BUZZ! BUZZ!

"What is that?" Ant cried. "It is big and black, with a voice like thunder. I must hide," Ant cried. "What can I hide under?"

"Well, look what I see!" said Tom. "Same old bee in that same old rose. He was here yesterday. And he is here today.

"Buzz, buzz, bee," said Tom. "Please go away."

"Swing, swing, sway, sway," said Ant. "I can't hold on to this tree all day. Help! Help! There I go! Down into space. Such a long, long way!

"Oh! I am lucky. Right into a bed of soft, furry hay."

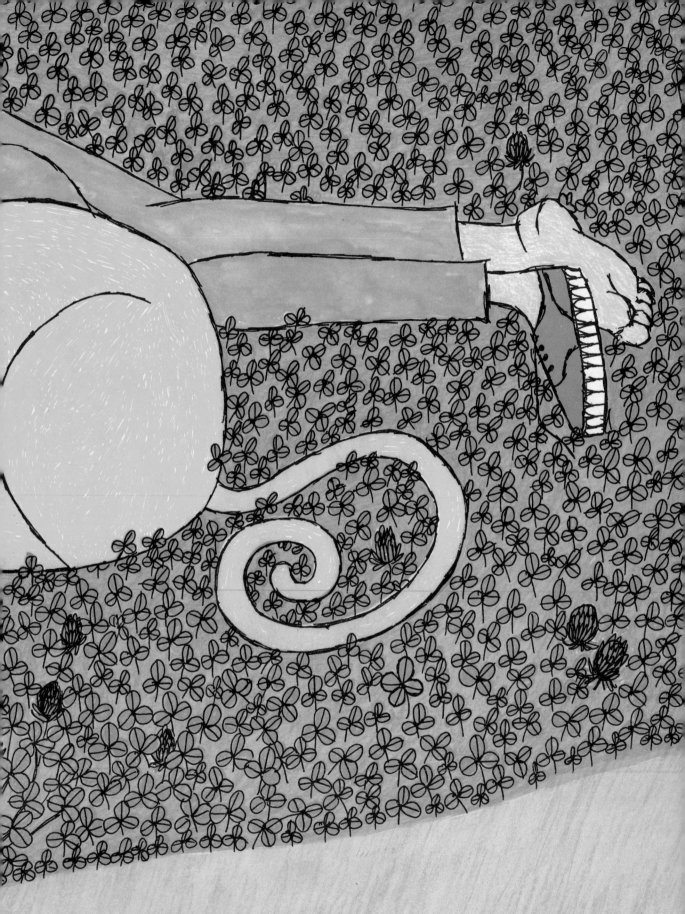

"Hello, cat," said Tom. "Do you want to play? What?
You want to sleep today? Same old sleepy cat," said Tom.

"I'm so tired," said Ant. "I'll just dig down a little way. And take a nap in this nice, soft hay."

JUMP! BUMP!
"Goodness," said Ant, "stay still, hay. Don't run away. I'll fall off. I'd better slide off, anyway. But what's below? I don't know. Oh, oh...."

"Look at cat," said Tom. "Look at him jump and run. Same old jump. Same old run. Cats don't do anything new that's fun."

"Where am I now?" whispered Ant. "It is wet and cold. It is black as ink. It's a great, rough lake!" cried Ant. "I can't swim a stroke! I know I will sink."

"Now, where I'd like to be," said Tom, "is down by the sea. I would swim and float and sail a boat.

"But all that is here," said Tom, "is that same old puddle. It's too little for a ship. It's too little for a dip. Silly, same old puddle."

"Saved," said Ant. "Saved by a raft with a nice dry floor. Oh, if only the wind will blow it to shore," said Ant. "Please, please . . . oh, thank you, breeze."

"Is that a stamp?" asked Tom. "Or could it be a piece of a letter that came for me?

"No, it's not a stamp, and the writing's so small, I can't read any of the words at all. It can't be for me. Silly old piece of paper."

Ant said, "I smell something sweet. And, oh, how I want something good to eat.

"What is this I see? A great big hill of sweetness. Enough for me ... and for my father and mother, my sisters and brothers, for every ant I know. But I can't make it move. I can't make it go.

"I know!" said Ant. "I'll get others to help me. How excited they'll be."

"Nothing to do," said Tom. "Nothing new. Even some candy or strawberry ice would be nice.

"Is that a piece of candy? Yes . . . but it's just a crumb. It's not even as big as the nail on my thumb."

"Here I am," called Ant. "Can you hear me, father? Do you see me, mother? Shall I tell you, sister? You won't believe it, brother!"

And Ant said:
"I walked a long way.
I saw a steep wall.
I climbed a great tree.

A beast almost ate me.
And then—what a fall!

The hay that caught me
moved like an earthquake.

So, I took a big leap
right into a lake.
It was black as ink,
and I can't swim or float.

I was going to sink
when along came a boat
(or, rather, a raft),
and I climbed on to it.

It took me to land
before I knew it.
And what did I find
when I reached the shore

but a hill of sweetness,
enough for us...
and for hundreds more!"

"Here I am," said Tom, "still in the same old spot. And it's still just as hot as it was yesterday.

"I can close my eyes," said Tom, "or look at the sky, or watch those silly old ants hurrying by. But what else is there to do?" asked Tom. "Not a thing to do that is fun and new."

"What a day," said Ant.
"Excitement and tears. I won't forget it
for years and years!"